Amelia's

MUST-KEEP

RESOLUTIONS

FOR THE

BEST YEAR EVER!

by Marissa Moss

(except all resolutions absolutely
100% made, worked at, and kept
by amelia for fun all year long!)

...l here   Simon & Schuster Books for   and, of course,
here!

Young Readers

New York   London   Toronto   Sydney

↙ and here ↗

It's almost the New Year and I'm all set with a year's worth of resolutions. This year I'm REALLY going to keep them too! Because this year I'm not going to make the kinds of resolutions that everyone makes and no one keeps, like promising not to eat any more junk food or to be nicer to my incredibly annoying sister, Cleo. I'm not going to solemnly resolve to always remember to bring my gym clothes home to wash — I mean, you don't know what stinky IS until you have to wear gym clothes left to rot in your locker for two weeks!! Because even though I WANT to remember, I know I'll forget sometimes.

gym locker with sweaty, smelly clothes — you can TASTE the rancid fumes before you even open the door!

You think something REALLY horrible is rotting in there, but it's your clothes and you have to WEAR them!

This is my first New Year in middle school, so I really want these resolutions to count. These have got to be the BEST resolutions ever! I want to think of stuff that's fun and easy to remember, but still gives you a sense of accomplishing something, like I resolve to give Cleo a new nickname whenever she gets on my nerves. Now, that's something I can do and feel good about!

Usually I call Cleo "Jelly Roll Nose" for obvious reasons, but I can be inspired to think up new titles, like the Queasy Queen of Car Sickness.

So here goes — my first resolution is to REALLY, TRULY, ABSOLUTELY, UNCONDITIONALLY, 100% keep all the resolutions I make in this notebook.

I raise my right hand and take the Oath of Resolution — I resolve to be resolved this year!

Resolution-to-be-kept-for-sure #1

I'm going to make the rest of 6th grade better with 14 easy steps to less stress.

One more week till winter vacation is over and school starts again. I want to begin with a clean slate. I'm <u>not</u> going to make the same mistakes I made last year. (If I make mistakes, at least they should be new ones.)

1) I solemnly swear to sit near the front of the class.

someone always makes a bunny shadow

Last year I sat in the back and when we saw movies or slides, I could hardly see anything. And when an author came to talk about how to make books, all I saw was hair!

I was an expert on the backs of people's heads — booooring!

Lunch Mom packs ↓

apple — how healthy ↓

peanut butter oozing out ↓

sandwich — one of four kinds Mom knows how to make: cheese, peanut butter, turkey, or stinky tuna salad (I HATE smelling like a fish all day!)

P-U! Fish breath ↓

two cookies—not too many

Lunch I will pack ↓

container of cold left-over spaghetti—yum! ↑

at least four cookies—different kinds, too ↑

crackers and cheese to make my own sandwich →

chips (the best part) →

2) I take an oath always to have at least <u>two</u> sharpened pencils at all times.

I always write and think better with a sharp, sharp tip. If the pencil is blunt and blocky, then my ideas are all clunky and globby.

3) I promise to pack my own lunch — then I <u>know</u> it will be good.

apple (well, I <u>do</u> want to be healthy) →

No more Chef's Surprise for me! ←

On my book covers I'll use stickers ↓

My English book will look like the solar system — it will be out of this world! →

My math book will be a really hard maze — will the numbers ever find their way out? →

4) I pledge to decorate my book covers the BEST I can.

5) I will never, ever wear an itchy turtleneck when I have to give an oral report.

sweaty fingers tugging at sweaty turtleneck →

throat feels all dry and choky with all that cloth around it →

it feels like the lump in my throat will never go away →

My social studies book will be a jungle — it's a jungle out there!

and rubber stamps ↓

6) I will definitely try to get to school early so I can see my friends before class starts.

Leah →

I can start the day right by talking ← with Leah and Carly — that always puts me in a good mood.

carly ↓

7) I vow never to write a boring book report again.

a big snooze ↓

Last year, one report was so boring, I fell asleep reading it for spelling mistakes. →

Z Z Z Z

yum, spicy! ↓

This year I'll add lots of spice, like I could write a report as if two people were arguing about the book or as if I were writing a review for a newspaper or as if I were one of the characters talking about what happens to me in the book.

I'll even decorate my binder with lanyard key chains

and rainbow pencils ↓

8) I promise, cross my heart, to return all my library books on time, so I'll always get to check out new ones.

and neon markers ↓ ★

OVERDUE! PAY NOW OR YOU MAY NEVER BOOKS FOR YOU!

Smell a fish—P-U! go back 2

sunny day— go ahead 1

You get a letter— go again

Cloudy day— go back 3

Miss the bus— back to start

9) I will try, try, try to do my homework FIRST THING after school, so I won't ever have to get up early the next morning to finish it.

z z z z z z z

Once Mom woke me up at 5:30! In the morning! It was still cold and dark outside. Even the birds were asleep. I wanted to stay in my warm, cozy bed — the last thing I wanted was to sit on a cold kitchen chair and face a sheet of math problems.

Slip on a banana peel— go back 4

Have a snack— lose a turn

10) I vow to care only about my grades, not about what other kids get.

Whaddya get, huh?

giraffe neck, stretching to see →

I hate it when other kids snoop and try to see my mistakes.

I don't ever want to be like this!

A on your test— move ahead 3

Hole in your sock— go back 2

Mud on shoes— go back 3

STOP lose a turn

Take a bathroom break— lose a turn

11) I resolve to draw in my notebook if no one lets me eat lunch with them and I feel left out.

In elementary school this worked. Last year when no one would play four-square or jump rope with me, I took some colored chalk and drew a gigantic hopscotch all around the edge of the whole playground. It was like a huge board game, only you threw a pebble, hopped to the square it landed on, and then did what that square said. It was so cool, even the boys wanted to join in. I had the whole school hopping!

Start

Try to throw the pebble on a good square

Peanut butter sticks to the roof of your mouth— lose a turn

Mom packs a cupcake in your lunch— go again

Dog eats homework— back to Start

Get sick — need a pill— lose a turn

Movie in class— go ahead 3

12) I vow not to cry if I get stuck in right field again in softball.

The ball never comes to right field — NOT EVER! Once I was so bored, I didn't even notice that my side had gone in to bat and I stayed in the outfield the whole period. No one even noticed I was missing.

13) I earnestly declare I will do at least FIVE full sit-ups for the Presidential Physical Fitness test.

I hope I can do this. (I'll practice, I promise.)

I can do this. I can do this. I can do this.

For all this effort, not moving somehow ↗

14) I pledge to be nice to a new kid because I remember all too well how it feels to be the new kid in class.

I'll bring extra cookies to offer to the new kid. If there is nobody new, I'll just eat them myself.

I couldn't resist — well one cookie is still a nice gift. →

And that's just the beginning! I hereby solemnly swear, pledge, promise, and declare to make more must-keep resolutions for the best year ever!

Resolution-to-be-kept-for-sure # 2

I resolve to find new ways to have fun in the snow this winter and new ways <u>not</u> to be cold, wet, and miserable.

green circle
(or easy)
trails
↓

I have my own list of ways to make winter more fun. → SNOW DOS

the path
to the snack
shop

1. Do drink hot chocolate often (marshmallows are optional).

Ah! The best part of the day!

← this, not this →

2. Do catch snowflakes on the tip of your tongue.

I spend more time on my rear than in gear!

Following behind Cleo — she clears a W I D E path

3. Do <u>stand</u> on your snowboard instead of <u>sitting</u> in the snow.

But if you <u>do</u> fall, land here. →

Whee! This is easy!

4. Do make your snowmen distinctive.

not this   but this   or this
↓   ↓   ↓

sliding downhill
on your bottom

Oops!

SNOW DON'TS

Hey!

1. Don't drop anything from the ski lift.

2. Don't use snowboarding lingo unless you know what it means.

I like to ollie on the trolley, but I hit a lolly and, by golly, it made me fall-y!

↑ Snowboarders have cool names for their tricks, but these aren't it!

black diamond (or <u>hard</u>) trails ↓

3. Don't snowboard, ski, or **go** sledding with wet hair — EVER! And don't drink anything cold while you're outside — you'll regret it!

chatter chatter

<u>real</u> brain freeze

My legs are like sacks of wet sand!

↑ the steps up to your cabin after a day on the slopes

4. <u>Don't</u> give up — no matter how much you fall.

Look on the bright side — I'm in the perfect position to make a snow angel!

I guess these socks are permanently attached now.

↑ getting out of wet snow clothes

Resolution-to-be-kept-for-sure #3

I'm going to make Valentine's Day a fun holiday any way I can!

I love Valentine's Day. I love making cards, getting cards, and eating cards (well, the candy _in_ them). Last year was especially fun. We all knew it was our last time to have a Valentine's Day class party. In middle school you have to figure out your own way to make it feel like a holiday. I bet Carly will wear heart earrings.

Carly is really into wearing valentine clothes.

socks with hearts

Carly has a lot of Valentine-type jewelry.

she wore all of these last February.

Last year Shawna joined our class, and Carly felt bad for her because she was so new, she probably wouldn't get any valentines. I know how it feels to move in the middle of the year because I did it myself. I sat next to Shawna at lunch and she told me that she'd already moved twice in one year. That was worse than me! I hoped she could stay this time.

Shawna, staring at her desk — she didn't know who to talk to.

pink jellies

Shawna was really nice, and when I said I'd never tasted sweet potato pie, she traded her piece to me for my ordinary ginger snaps.

For my valentine, I used glitter.

real scraps of lace from Mom's sewing box →

heart sequins →

Carly wore heart beads and a pink shirt. ↓

Naya wore a red velvet dress with a collar that looks like a doily. ↓

Where did Susie even find a pink-and-red striped shirt? ↓

Even Hilary, the bully, looked sweet with her heart shirt.

Shawna gave me a valentine even sweeter than her pie!

FR (chint: tail = end)

I was worried she wouldn't even want to stay if she had a lonely Valentine's day, so I decided to rescue Shawna. I made her the biggest, fanciest card ever. It even popped up.

I couldn't wait to see her face when she got my card. I imagined that she'd be so excited, she'd hug me, like I saved her or something. Then she'd really like living here. It was the closest I could come to being a hero.

Oh, Super Valentine, thank you, thank you, thank you!

Now, this is a Valentine's Day outfit!

It's nothing, really. All in a day's work.

I left my card on Shawna's desk, but there was already a pile there. It turned out Carly made an extra-special valentine too. And so did eight other kids. I didn't get to be a hero, but Shawna sure was happy. I guess that shows it's not the party that makes Valentine's Day fun — it's the friends. And I've got great ones!

I'm still going to miss those pink cupcakes. ↓

I don't resolve to keep my room clean (although I know that's what Mom wants me to promise). But at least I'll figure out what the mess in my room means. A room can tell you a lot about a person, and I want to be able to read my room better than anyone else.

These are some easy guides for room interpretation:

My dream room would have:

a skylight (with a telescope, of course!)

a secret compartment behind the bookcase.

my own vending machine full of junk food.

The oldest thing in m room is:

the teddy bear I had when I was a baby.

the handprint I made when I was in kindergarten.

the fossilized Cheerios under the bed.

My favorite room decoration is:

↑
my collection of
glass animals,
neatly dusted.

↑
the glow-in-the-
dark stars on my
ceiling.

Bloop! Bloop!

↑
my lava lamp
if I can ever
find where I
put it!

Other clues to Room Reading:

It's simpler than figuring out
what those lines in your palm →
mean.

↑
If the trash has
a lot of tissues
in it, you have a
baaaaad cold.

If there are lots of
spiderwebs, you don't
have to worry about
flies, but you need to
dust!

↑
If the water in
the fish bowl is
green, have pity
on your poor fish
and CHANGE THE
WATER!

↑
Unless you're going
for the haunted house
look, in which case
you need MORE webs.

↑
If your books are
in alphabetical order,
you should help out at
your local library.

↑
If your colored pencils
have bite marks on
them, then you have a
taste for art!

Resolution-to-be-kept-for-sure #5

I resolve to find SOMETHING good about each substitute teacher. It's not their fault — they don't know what the class is used to — and it's definitely not their fault if they're replacing a teacher you really, really like.

I love Ms. Reilly, my science teacher, but she got a grant to study in INDIA so we had a substitute for a whole month — good for her, bad for us. I tried to have an open mind about it. I promised Carly I wouldn't draw any evil witch pictures of the new teacher and I wouldn't make any voodoo dolls.

Then she came, Mrs. Grund. She was just like her name — a grunt. The first thing she did was read us all these rules. She didn't smile once. A whole month with her! GRUNT!!

cardboard strips ←   brads →   rolls of foil ↘   boxes of nails

This is junk — not science equipment! →

I hated what Mrs. Grund was doing to the classroom. There were boxes of junk blocking the bookshelf. What was more important, books or bits of wood and wire? And what was all that stuff for, anyway? Was Mrs. Grund going to build some kind of torture device? It was torture enough having her for a substitute.

Mrs. Grund ↓

mouth pinched tight →

looooooong list of rules →

If don det you to lea neigh with no ye no n no d

I wasn't the only one who didn't like our substitute. Lots of kids were acting up.

Half the class didn't pay attention at all.

George fell asleep when the rules were read

Mrs. Grund said she was sorry to block the bookcase, but she was collecting things for our first science project. I love science, but what could come out of junk? I finally got to 6th grade, and it was like being in kindergarten, hammering nails into wood and calling it sculpture.

side view → oooh! what beautiful art! nails form a smiley face — how creative! top view

At least Carly was there

Raoul brought his pet frog the first day

All that junk turned out to be not so junky. We put it all together and made a telegraph. It was soooo cool! The next week we made rockets. (I couldn't wait to see what kind of stuff Mrs. Grund brought for that!)

Moe sneaking snacks — he smells like popcorn

I LOVE making inventions
cardboard taped down   foil
tap this down and then the brad taps the nail, making a clicking sound
← cardboard nailed down
wood   foil   ← wires →   battery   nail wrapped with wire   brad   wood
this becomes an electromagnet — wow!

Brandon kept on burping loudly.

Mrs. Grund was still strict, but she had good ideas for projects. And she really taught me something — about substitutes as well as science. I can't wait to try experimenting on my next substitute. I know I'll learn something!

bunch of kids were passing notes back and forth.

Have a good weekend, class. Come back Monday prepared to rock and roll — or is that roll your rocket?

head full of good ideas

eyebrows that are happy

friendly smiling mouth

Resolution-to-be-kept-for-sure #6

WATCH OUT

FOR THESE MOLDY OLDIES!
↓

↑
the dangling rubber spider

↑
the dribble glass

ptoo!

↑
the squirting nickel

↑
the innocent-looking but super-hot candy

CK ME ← the stupid sign stuck on someone's back

I want to be the one playing the tricks this year!

Last year I was all set for April Fool's. I hid a whoopee cushion under the seat of Cleo's chair so that she'd have a nice surprise at breakfast. And for Mom, I set her alarm clock to go off a half hour earlier. Then I checked my room for any possible Cleo traps — all clear! I wanted to be the trickster, not the tricked.

No one liked my morning jokes. Mom was extra-grouchy (who thought thirty minutes of sleep would matter?).

P.U.! Cleo, did you HAVE to? And while we're eating?

Very funny, Amelia. Hardy har har.

Cleo didn't appreciate my joke, but I thought it was hilarious!

Then at school, I played a great joke on Carly.

Wow! My lucky day!

She saw a dollar bill on the ground. Just as she bent down to pick it up...

corner to hide behind
↓

I yanked it away!

← dollar bill attached to fishing wire

She thought it was such a good trick, she wanted to try it.

"Please let me borrow the dollar! Please, please, pleeeease!"

"I want to use it on Max. He always brags about finding money."

↑
gum that turns teeth black (SMILE!)

So I let Carly have the money after all (no yanking away this time). I don't need a prop to play a trick anyway. At lunch, I told Leah she had mayonnaise on her face.

↑
bug in plastic ice cube

"Here?" "Nope."

"Here?" "Naw."

"Here?" "Uh uh."

Finally I said "April Fool! There's NOTHING there!" Leah burst out laughing. "I was sure there was," she said, "because you have a glob of mustard on your face." I thought she was trying my own joke back on me, but it was true.

↑
rubber pencil

When I got home, there was a package for me — from Nadia!

How sweet of her! It wasn't even close to my birthday!

I opened it and inside was a tin of candy. At least, I thought it was candy.

SPROOING!

snakey things springing out of can

First I was startled, then I laughed. Okay, I did get tricked, but only once. This ye   ll b even trickier!

Resolution-to-be-kept-for-sure #7

Fun
Iguana
Facts
↓

yum, smells good!

↑
Iguanas smell with their tongues like snakes do.

Achooo!

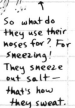

↑
So what do they use their noses for? For sneezing! They sneeze out salt — that's how they sweat.

I gotta go!

↑
Some people potty-train their iguanas!

Someday, somehow I'll prove to Mom I'm responsible enough for a pet so can I __PLEASE__ have one?

I tried to do this before but it didn't work the way I planned.

Mrs. Grund asked if one of us would take Ivana, the class iguana, home for spring break. I really had to beg, but finally Mom said _I_ could do it! The only condition was that I had to keep Ivana in my bedroom, because Mom didn't want to see her — reptiles give her the creeps.

Ivana was a reptile, but she wasn't creepy. She was kind of cute.

She looked like a tiny dinosaur or a miniature dragon.

nice warm eyes

↑ friendly smile

If you want creepy, the class next to ours had a Red Hills salamander. It looked like a slimy giant worm — yucch!

Ivana looked happy in my room. Since she was cold-blooded, she needed a light on all the time to keep her warm. I hadn't slept with a night-light for _years_, but I didn't mind having a nice iguana glow. It was kind of like a lava lamp.

I made a prehistoric jungle background for Ivana's cage — now she _really_ looks like a dinosaur. →

← Don't forget to plug in the light!

I became an iguana expert. I knew how to trim their nails and how to make their favorite salad (vegetables _and_ fruit). I wished Mom would see what a great job I was doing and let me have my _own_ iguana — or some other pet that didn't have scales.

iguana paw prints (Or are they footprints? I know — they're claw prints!)

examined the carpet for claw prints — no luck!

Then something terrible happened! I put Ivana in an old shoe box while I was cleaning out her cage, and she must have tipped the box over, because she was GONE! I HAD to find her before Mom got home or she'd never trust me again!

I tried not to panic. The situation called for a clear head. I would use my detective skills and iguana knowledge to solve the Mystery of the Vanishing iguana.

Plus Mrs. Grund and the kids at school would be furious!

Mrs. Grund

Carls

Max

← angry faces glaring at me

Cleo laughing at me ←

Ha, ha, serves her right!

set out lettuce bait, but no one bit.

looked other places food left out.

I looked everywhere and time was running out.

I got on the floor for an iguana's eye view. Where would I go, if I were an iguana?

lost penny

rubber band

cracker crumbs

dust bunnies

cold kitchen floor ↗

always ts in bed, there nothing re.

! Under e bed, pied nething en and aly.

If I were Ivana, I'd be someplace warm. I checked the oven — luckily no baked iguana pie there. Then I remembered — it was warm behind the refrigerator because its motor was warm. When I got closer, I heard a sneeze and, sure enough, there was Ivana!

She looked happy to see me.

eye to eye with an iguana ↓

ps! + a stinky o sock.

When Mom came home, I told her about Ivana's escape. She said it was a good thing I found her or I'd never get a pet. But I was back to ZERO when it came to proving responsibility. I need another chance. I want to borrow Ivana again and next time, there'll be NO escapes!

Resolution-to-be-kept-for-sure #8

Mom's working on cleaning equipment for the space station. Maybe I can invent my own galactic cleaners.

star polish—add shine to your star's sparkle

high-power black hole vacuum—sucks up dirt, dust, and everything else

asteroid cleanser—scrubs out even the toughest stains

You always hear the expression if you've got a lemon, make lemonade. Just once, I want to turn a mistake into a good thing!

Last year on Take Your Kid to Work Day, Mom took Cleo and me to her lab. Cleo doesn't care about cool science stuff. She was just glad to miss school, so she didn't even bother with a tour.

Cleo stayed glued to the cookies and lemonade. The other kids had better hurry or there won't be anything left.

She was conducting her own experiments — ① how much could she cram into her mouth at once, ② how loudly could she chomp, an ③ how messy she could be

science in action↗

That didn't stop Mom from being excited about explaining stuff to me. She figures out what kinds of metals work best in satellites and the International Space Station.

She showed me a row of beakers with metal rods sitting in chemical solut

I'm testing a new super-light aluminum alloy to see if we can use it in cleaning equipment in the space station.

These are all different chemicals. I'll examine the rods for corrosion later.

I wanted to see if there was anything corroding already, so I ___ d over for a closer look

DISAS ER!

Oh, no!

GULP!

I didn't mean to, but somehow my lemonade splashed right into one of Mom's chemicals!

Too bad it wasn't already a yellow liquid so that Mom wouldn't suspect anything. There was no way I could hide *this*!

strange
ravitational
ull yanked
e lemonade
ght out of
my glass.

I had to think of <u>something</u> — quick! I didn't know what to do. Then Mom noticed.

Funny, this solution is cloudy and yellow now. It was clear a minute ago.

Maybe a bird overhead had to go to the bathroom.

"A bird <u>indoors</u>?" Mom wanted to know. "Amelia?"

"Did you know Cleo can spit <u>really</u> far?" I asked desperately.

There was no getting around it, I had to tell the truth.

monade
roplets
ndensed
nto the
eaker.
ley, it
asn't my
fault.

Um, Mom, I'm really sorry, but . . .

You <u>what</u>?!

I wanted to sink into the floor.

Mom was mad at first, but then she thought it was funny.

"Maybe you can just say you're testing a new cle.   " I said, "a lemony-fresh one!" I didn't t   emon into lemonade, but it was close   need another chance!

Hey, this rocket smells great!

Resolution-to-be-kept-for-sure #9

I resolve to do SOMETHING I've never done before and make a drawing out of it. Bungee-jumping? Eating squid? Who knows!

Last spring Carly and I went to a dog show. Neither of us has a dog, but we thought it would be fun to look at all the different breeds and pick out which one we'd want, if we could ever convince our parents to let us have a puppy.

It was amazing to see all the different kinds of dogs, from the teeny-tiny Pomeranian to the horse-sized Great Dane.

Some dogs at the show were getting the deluxe treatment!

FWOOO!

dog being blow-dried — now there's more hair than dog!

dog with a manicure — I mean, pedicure

They don't even look like the same species — more like a hamster next to a pony.

I call dogs your size a snack!

He could eat the Pomeranian in one bite!

One paw is bigger than the whole tiny dog!

That made me think — there's no other animal that comes in as many varieties as dogs do. Carly said that's because dogs are the pets that most look like their owners... or the owners look like the dogs. I'm not sure which way it works, but we saw the resemblance over and over again at the dog show.

That gave me a great idea! I made a chart of people I know and the dogs that match them.

dog getting its eyebrows and beard trimmed

Here's a leash — sometimes I wonder who's pulling whom.

Cleo

shar-pei — yes, there really is a dog with a jelly-roll nose!

Mom

corgi — short legs and short hair with ears that hear everything

Nadia

cocker spaniel — big brown eyes, silky hair, and a sweet face, just like Nadia

Gigi

collie — long nose, elegant face, mane of hair, and loyal, too!

Max

beagle — way too much energy packed into one body

Mrs. Kravitz

Bedlington terrier — Brillo-pad hair and a bleating bark

Carly

Poodle — smart and stylish

And here's the perfect dog for me...

...a mutt — a little bit of this, a little bit of that, a dog with energy and a mind of its own!

TOP DOG

It was inspiring to see all the dogs and draw them — you never know where you'll get ideas, especially when you do something new. I wonder what it will be this year!

Resolution-to-be-kept-for-sure #10

I promise not to ruin vacation time by doing <u>any</u> work. That's what the rest of the year is for!

All vacation time is great, but SUMMER is the best. That's when I finally get to do all the great summer stuff I've been waiting for all year.

IN CAMP

WHEN I'M NOT IN CAMP
↓

swimming — I get to really work on my diving

building a treehouse

making lanyards—lanyard key chains, lanyard bracelets, lanyard bookmarks, lanyard EVERYTHING!

walking around barefoot and feeling grass between my toes

staying up late reading because there's no school tomorrow

hikes, which means dirty, dusty shoes

practicing double dutch with Carly

concocting interesting science experiments (DO NOT EAT!)

un-favorite summer stuff
↓

The problem is sometimes I try to cram in <u>too</u> much fun. I remember last June I was so happy to have no school, I couldn't stop myself — after hiking, swimming, tie-dying, and candle-making, I was too tired even to read a comic book. By July I was exhausted! <u>Something</u> had to change.

bug bites—how come bugs never bite cleo? if I smelled like her, would they stop biting me? would it be worth it?

← scraped knees—ouch! That Mercurochrome stings!

I went to the pool with Carly in the morning, but after that I decided to TAKE A BREAK. I needed a vacation from all that vacation. So that afternoon I planned to do ABSOLUTELY NOTHING! When I got home, I made myself a snack of summery watermelon and summery lemonade and lay down in the hammock in the backyard.

I was going to read, but I just lay there and watched the leaves flutter in the breeze. I listened to birds trill and dogs bark. I felt my hair tickling my cheek and the warm sun between my toes. I breathed in the green afternoon air and smelled dried grass and soft, baked dirt. If I could put it all in a bottle and carry it with me, I could have summer whenever I wanted. I felt summer right down to my toes. It was just the kind of vacation I needed and the best day I had all summer!

essence of summer

sunshine

puffy clouds

light, warm breezes

fluttering leaves

dried grass and dandelions

Resolution-to-be-kept-for-sure #11

I want to learn something that most people don't think of bothering with, like knowing at least 10 constellations or how to whittle, something fun and old-fashioned.

Last summer I went camping with Carly and her family. They all knew a lot about nature. Carly could name a dozen constellations and her brothers were expert bird-watchers. I wanted to be good at something too.

They can tell a finch from a flycatcher.

I thought a flycatcher was a baseball player!

At least I can tell scary stories around the campfire.

Carly showed me the constellation Cassiopeia.

Carly's brother told a story he said was true about how a woman was attacked by a mountain lion last year in this same park. Carly didn't believe him, but her other brother said he'd read about it, too.

They can identify a yellow-bellied sapsucker. All I can identify is a yellow rubber ducky.

fact or fiction?

real or a dream?

Sleeping in a tent was hard enough — it felt like the ground was sprouting sharp rocks under my sleeping bag — but I kept thinking I heard something rustling outside. Something like a large animal. Something like... a mountain lion?

Ground should be flat

not sharp!

NIGHT NOISES

I didn't know bugs could chew so loudly. KEE-RUNCH!

EERRAGGH EERRAGGH!

Frogs sounded like drums. BRRUPPUPPUP BRRUPPUPPUP

I kept my eyes on the ground today, looking for animal tracks. I was sure that after hearing all those noises last night, I'd find something.

hat were they omping nyway? Leaves? Gravel? Me?!

And I did — a great BIG paw print. I wanted to follow the

At first I thought it was a bear's, but it was too round.

That meant it had to be a MOUNTAIN LION'S!

tracks, but I also wanted to get as far away as possible. Before I could, there was a

RUSSSSSTTLE

in the bushes—like the night before! Something BIG was in there! And whatever it was, it was coming closer.

Yum! tasty uman!

EWOOOOSH!

A tawny beast burst through the bushes. Carly screamed — then started laughing. "It's not a mountain lion- it's a Great Dane!" she yelled. I was SO embarrassed (well, relieved, too). "It's big enough to be a mountain lion, so I was close," I said. "Anyway, people shouldn't take dogs camping — they'll scare away the wildlife." But that night, I was glad the dog was nearby. He was the one who got sprayed by a skunk — not us. And

ere's a wild nimal definitely DON'T ant to et near!

I'm friendly!

I learned a new animal track -the paw print of Canis Maximus or Giant Dog. By next summer I want to be an expert!

Resolution-to-be-kept-for-sure #12

I will NOT let my brain get soggy over the summer. I promise to use it in some fun way that has nothing to do with school. I can make my own mental calisthenics and build smart muscles.

Are you letting your brain go soft this summer? Does it feel like slogging through hip-high mud to squeeze out a thought? You'd better take this quiz to see if your thinking is crisp or soggy. A score of one or fewer correct answers means you've got some exercising to do!

POP QUIZ

Quick! Say Jell-O backward.

(But don't eat it backward!)

Huff, huff!

What's in the mountains, in the air we breathe, and even in the sea, but not in cities, deserts, or the country?

Oof!

Can it be fish?

We breathe fish?

Try again!

What do you break as soon as you say its name?

Oops! Clumsy me!

THING

Yes, but what thing exactly?

what's in green and orange but not in blue or purple?

What can crawl, run out, fly, and even stand still but NEVER sit or walk?

One, two, three...

Time's up!

What's the answer?

A baseball can be a fly ball or a walk—does that count?

No, it's not the rock-hard jelly beans under your bed—it's the color yellow!

What goes flip-splat, flip-splat, flip-splat, flip-splat, flip-splat, flip-splat, flip-splat, flip-splat?

An octopus making pancakes!

Even without a chin, I can do a chin-up!

hat gets igger ne more you take away?

↓

a hole

4. What is this a picture of?

And this?

Beats me! I never get modern art.

GOOD! crispy, crunchy brain

ANSWERS

BAD! mushy, lumpy brain

Feel that muscle!

1. Not trees, the color blue, or bugs — it's the letter **A**!

Gotcha!

I'm exhausted!

2. Silence! (Shhh! Even a whisper breaks silence — it's more fragile than glass.)

3. Time! Haven't you seen time fly before?

Time flies when you're having fun!

4. An egg reflected in a mirror.

Now I need a nap.

5. A pig seen from below.

I like what I see!

I just like giving people tests.

I'm much cuter seen THIS way!

It's much more fun to <u>make</u> tests instead of taking them. That's the kind of brain strain that isn't a pain!

Resolution - to - be - kept - for - sure # **13**

I resolve to be a better notebook writer. When I don't know what to write about, I'll look at this resolution and get some ideas.

1. Write about things that matter to you — and say why.

No!

"I read a book."

Yes!

"I read this great book about a boy who's a wizard. It was so exciting, I couldn't put it down!"

2. Give details!

No!

"It was hot."

Yes!

"It was so hot I felt like melted ice cream."

3. You don't have to write just about stuff you did. You can also write about what you're thinking or noticing.

"Did you ever notice how people have different kinds of noses?"

up nose   down nose   jelly roll nose   pig type nose

4. Or write about what you _feel_ and why.
(Sometimes writing it down helps you figure
out _why_ you feel that way.)

happy   sad   excited   scared   mad

5. If you've heard a funny story or joke,
pass it on.

Funny is good!

6. Sometimes pictures work better
than words.

For my mom's birthday I baked a cake.

I imagined it would look like this.

Hey, who sat on my cake?

But it turned out like this.

That's a great start. And when I don't know what
to write, I can ALWAYS draw something. Or do both
together — I love to make comics.

Resolution-to-be-kept-for-sure # 14

I will learn to cook something besides cookies. I want to know how to make real food even if it's something easy like macaroni and cheese. (That _is_ easy, isn't it?)

Aunt Lucy came to spend last Thanksgiving with us. I wanted to do something special since it was the first Thanksgiving her daughter, Raisa, had ever had. Aunt Lucy adopted her last year from a Russian orphanage. I'm sure there was no turkey _there_.

When they arrived, Mom started discussing recipes with Aunt Lucy, so I took Raisa outside to play and we had a tea party under the oak tree.

Mom is always nervous when we have family over. ↓

Let's see, did I forget anything now? Soy milk for Raisa, Lucy's favorite granola, clean towels — wait, I forgot the turkey!

Raisa set out some cookies and lemonade for the birds and squirrels. She wanted to feed them too. ↓

Mr. Bunny goes everywhere with her and eats everything. →

Raisa was 4 years old, but she didn't talk much. If you look at her face, though, you could see what she wanted to say.

↑
Aunt Lucy is Mom's complete opposite (like Cleo and me, I guess). She forgot to pack socks for Raisa because she didn't make a list the way mom did.

The acorns from the tree gave me an idea. Native Americans used to eat nuts lots of different ways. I found a recipe for nut mush on the Internet that could have been eaten at the first Thanksgiving. I thought it would be cool for Raisa to have it at _her_ first Thanksgiving. Mom said acorns would make everyone sick, so I decided to use walnuts instead.

You can use walnuts for art projects too! →

Thanksgiving Day the first thing I did was make my mush. It was a LOT of work grinding all those nuts. Mom finished the biscuits, sweet potatoes, and pumpkin pie in the time it took me to make one bowl of mush. I should've made macaroni and cheese instead— that's an all-American dish!

Finally everything was ready. The table looked beautiful.
↓

↑
Cleo was thankful Mom didn't make that awful Jell-o again.

↑
Mom was thankful we were all celebrating together.

↑
Lucy gave thanks for finding Raisa.

Raisa said "Thank you."

I just wanted us to stop thanking and start eating my nut mush.

After all the toasts, it was time to eat at last. Everyone took a BIG bite of mush.

Cleo, bolting for the bathroom ↳

mom, in mid-chew ↓

Aunt Lucy, trying to be polite ↳

Raisa, being honest →

Cleo ran from the table. Mom and Lucy sat there with their mouths full, not swallowing, and Raisa said, "Yuck!"

I tried it, and she was right — it was DISGUSTING! The mush was so gross, Raisa put the bowl outside on the ground. I thought she wanted it far away from her, but she said "Now the squirrels have Thanksgiving too!" I'm glad the squirrels enjoyed my cooking — someone needed to. Next time I want to make food people can eat — something besides cookies!

If I can keep all of my resolutions, this will definitely be the best year ever. I almost wish it was the year 2000 again because that was more than a new year — it was a new millenium. And these resolutions are millenium-worthy! I heard that some people thought it would be a **bad** beginning because computers would read "00" as "1900," not "2000." Of course, there weren't any problems, but I came up with a top-ten list of worst fears, kind of like anti-resolutions.

1) I could be stuck in an elevator FOREVER.

I bet people in the Middle Ages didn't worry like this when it was the year 1000.

← crowded with people wearing smelly perfumes and carrying bulging purses

It's stopping finally — at the 13th floor.

There is no 13th floor.

Now there is! Today's your lucky day.

2) The library would say I owe $1,382,643.84 in overdue fines.

angry librarian finger

My card will be shredded.

No more books for you — EVER!

3) The doctor would say I need all my shots AGAIN!

The records for your shots are gone. We'll just have to do them over.

Don't worry. It won't hurt MUCH.

MOM!

oh no, the new millennium— now horses and boats won't go any more. And will windmills still have power? Will the sun still set?

4) Microwave ovens would turn food into rubber.

BOING!

← follow the bouncing potato

oatmeal blob or new tire material

It was popcorn, now it can be used for earplugs.

the <u>real</u> changes →

↓

Everything from the previous year was instant ancient history.

↓

More number 2's were printed than number 1's. →

Now I'm number one!

My days are numbered.

5) TV stations everywhere would broadcast only the home shopping channel.

What a deal! →

This wonderful slicer/dicer/ricer/splicer can be <u>yours</u> for only $49.99! But hurry! Supplies <u>are</u> limited.

6) I'd get 6,000 copies of the same catalog in the mail.

And now, a song from the last millennium.

Oh, goody, my Modern Clothes catalog.

Day 1

Six <u>more</u> Modern Clothes catalogs?

Day 2

HELP!

Day 3

7) The only radio station I'd be able to get would be in Finnish.

Everyone became bi-centurions and bi-millenniums.

↓

Og sløgsk!

Yes, I'm from the last century and the last millennium!

8) Everyone's watch alarm would go off at the same time.

EEB EEB EEB EEB

BIP BIP

BEEP BEEP

Make them stop!

PEE DOO PEE DOO

OOOH OOOH OOOH OOOH

DIT DIT DIT DIT

I didn't even use a time machine.

9) Vending machines would pour out hot chocolate, but not the cup.

I'm getting that hot chocolate!

HOT

hot chocolate bloat

10) Parking meters would explode. (<u>That</u> would be fun!)

Aren't I amazing?! I've lived in two different centuries and I'm <u>still</u> so young!

I won the jackpot!

None of my anti-resolutions came true, but that doesn't mean I can't keep all of my positive resolutions, every single to-be-kept-for-sure one. I made some good ones — much easier to keep than promising to clean my room or wash my gym clothes — and much more fun!

I resolve to dedicate this notebook to all
the kids who love Amelia,

to Katherine, Georgia, Tamika, Tara Bradley,

and to everyone who reads these books!

SIMON & SCHUSTER BOOKS FOR YOUNG READERS
An imprint of Simon & Schuster Children's Publishing Division
1230 Avenue of the Americas, New York, New York 10020

Copyright © 2006 by Marissa Moss

SIMON & SCHUSTER BOOKS FOR YOUNG READERS
IS A TRADEMARK OF SIMON & SCHUSTER, INC.

Amelia® and the notebook design are
registered trademarks of Marissa Moss.

A Paula Wiseman Book
Book design by Amelia
(with help from Lucy Ruth Cummins)
The text for this book is hand-lettered.
Manufactured in the United States of America
2 4 6 8 10 9 7 5 3 1

CIP data for this book is available
from the Library of Congress.

ISBN-13: 978-1-4169-3361-8   ISBN-10: 1-4169-3361-1